MY 1ST GRAPHIC NOVEL

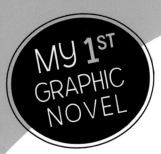

SECRET SCOOTER

My First Graphic Novels are published by Stone Arch Books
151 Good Counsel Drive, P.O. Box 669
Mankato, Minnesota 56002
www.stonearchbooks.com

Library of Congress Cataloging-in-Publication Data
Jones, Christianne C.
    Secret scooter / by Christianne C. Jones ; illustrated by Mary Sullivan.
    p. cm. — (My first graphic novel)
    ISBN 978-1-4342-1619-9 (library binding)
    1. Graphic novels. [1. Graphic novels. 2. Motor scooters—Fiction.]
I. Sullivan, Mary, 1958- ill. II. Title.
PZ7.7.J66Se 2010
741.5'973—dc22

                                        2008053373

Summary: Every day Jackson sees his dream scooter buzzing around town.
He is determined to catch it, no matter what it takes.

Creative Director: Heather Kindseth
Graphic Designer: Hilary Wacholz

Printed in the United States of America

MY 1ST GRAPHIC NOVEL

SECRET SCOOTER

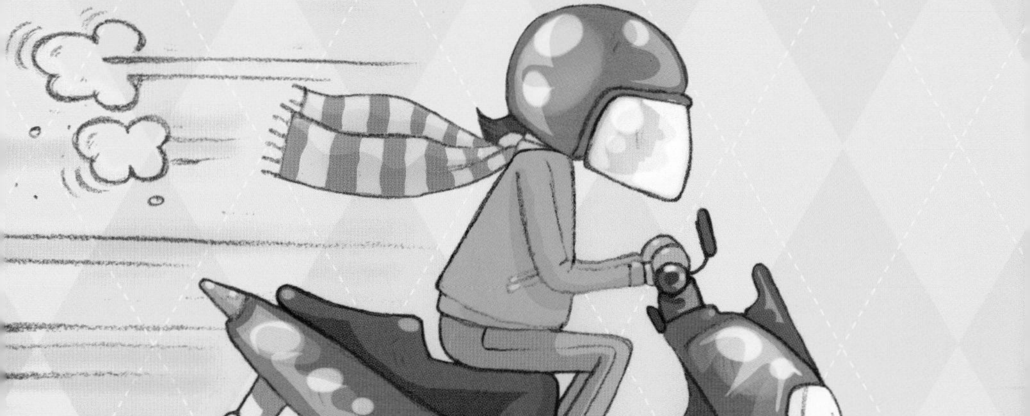

by Christianne C. Jones
illustrated by Mary Sullivan

STONE ARCH BOOKS
MINNEAPOLIS SAN DIEGO

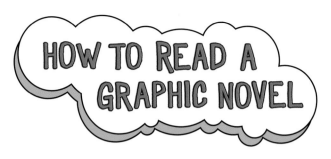

HOW TO READ A GRAPHIC NOVEL

Graphic novels are easy to read. Boxes called panels show you how to follow the story. Look at the panels from left to right and top to bottom.

Read the word boxes and word balloons from left to right as well. Don't forget the sound and action words in the pictures.

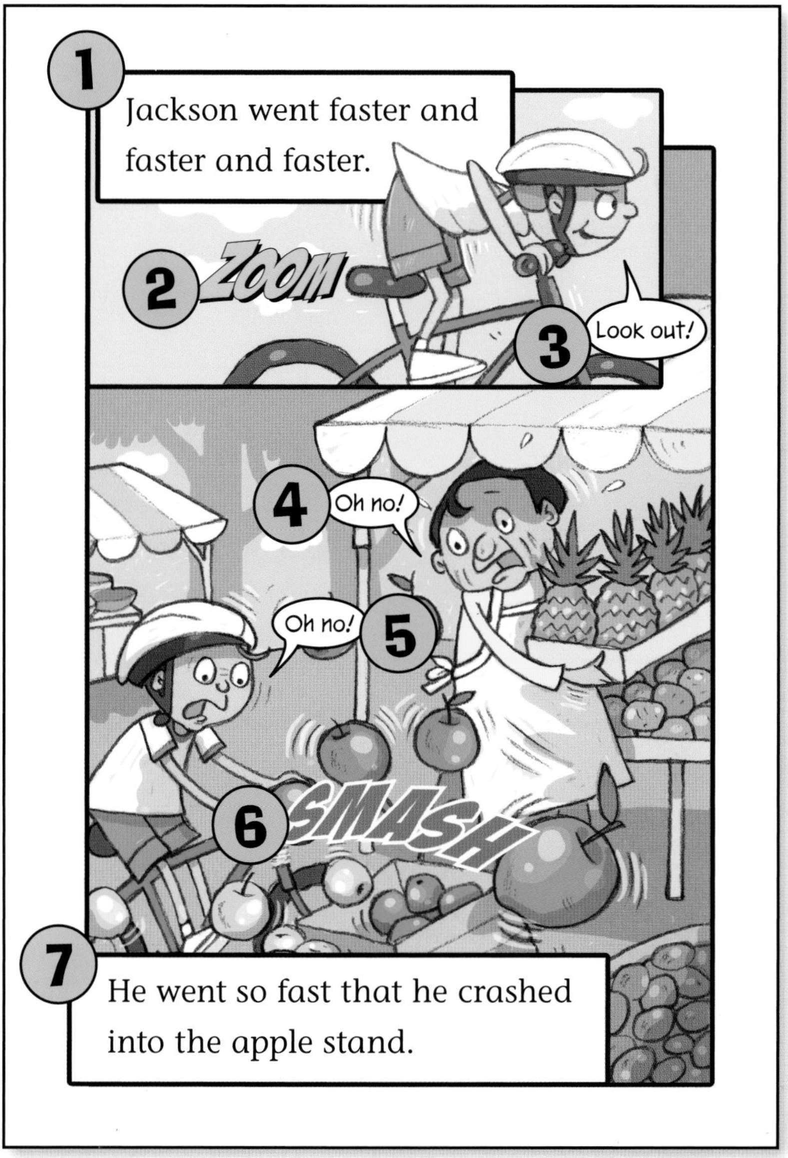
1
Jackson went faster and faster and faster.
2
ZOOM
3
Look out!
4
Oh no!
Oh no!
5
6
SMASH
7
He went so fast that he crashed into the apple stand.

The pictures and the words work together to tell the whole story.

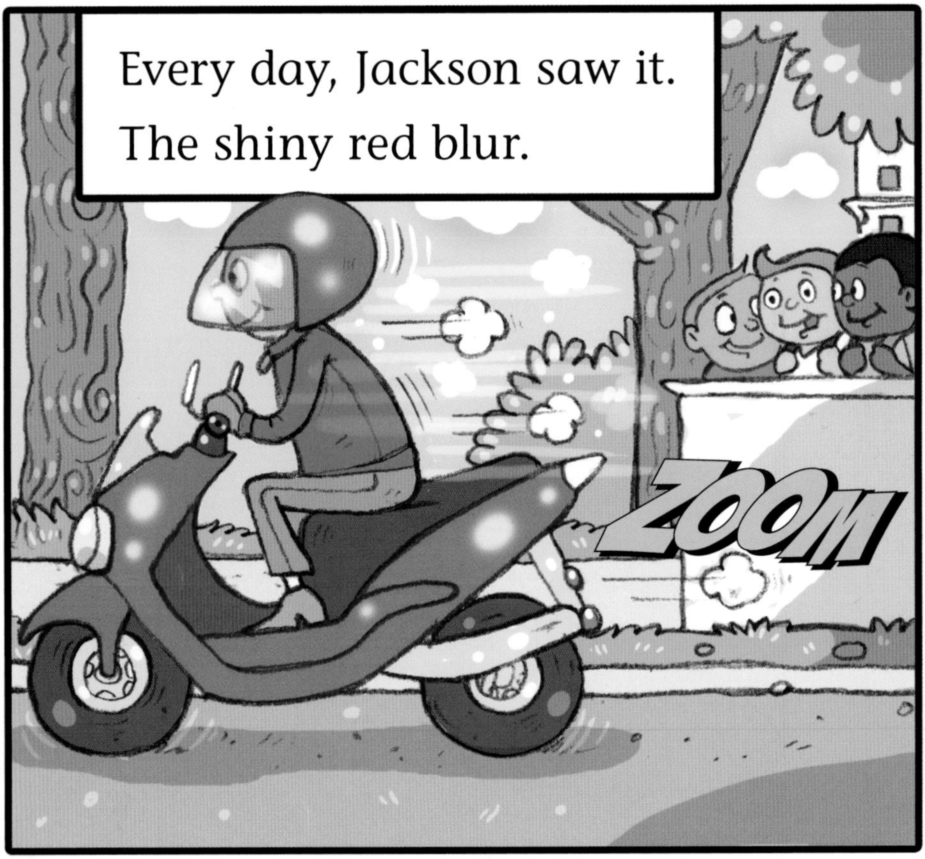
Every day, Jackson saw it.
The shiny red blur.
ZOOM

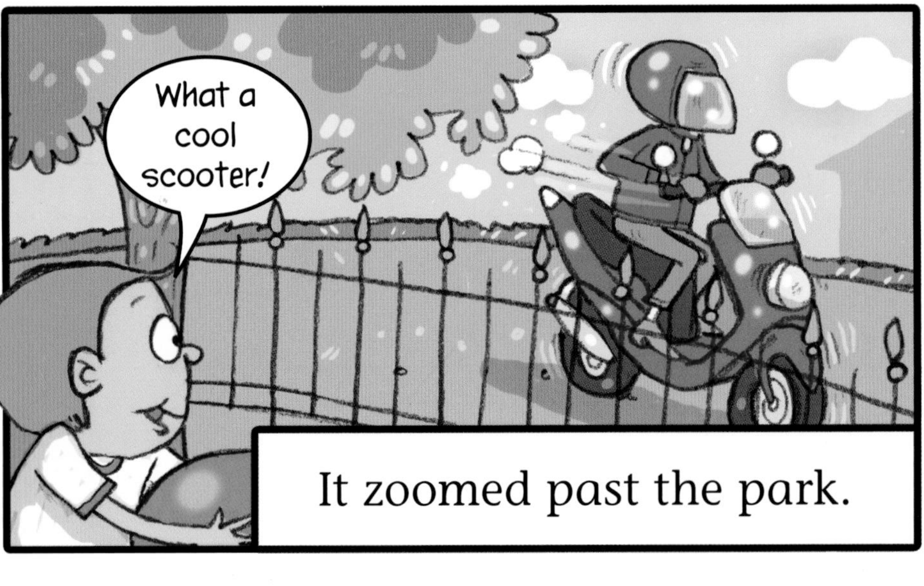
What a cool scooter!
It zoomed past the park.

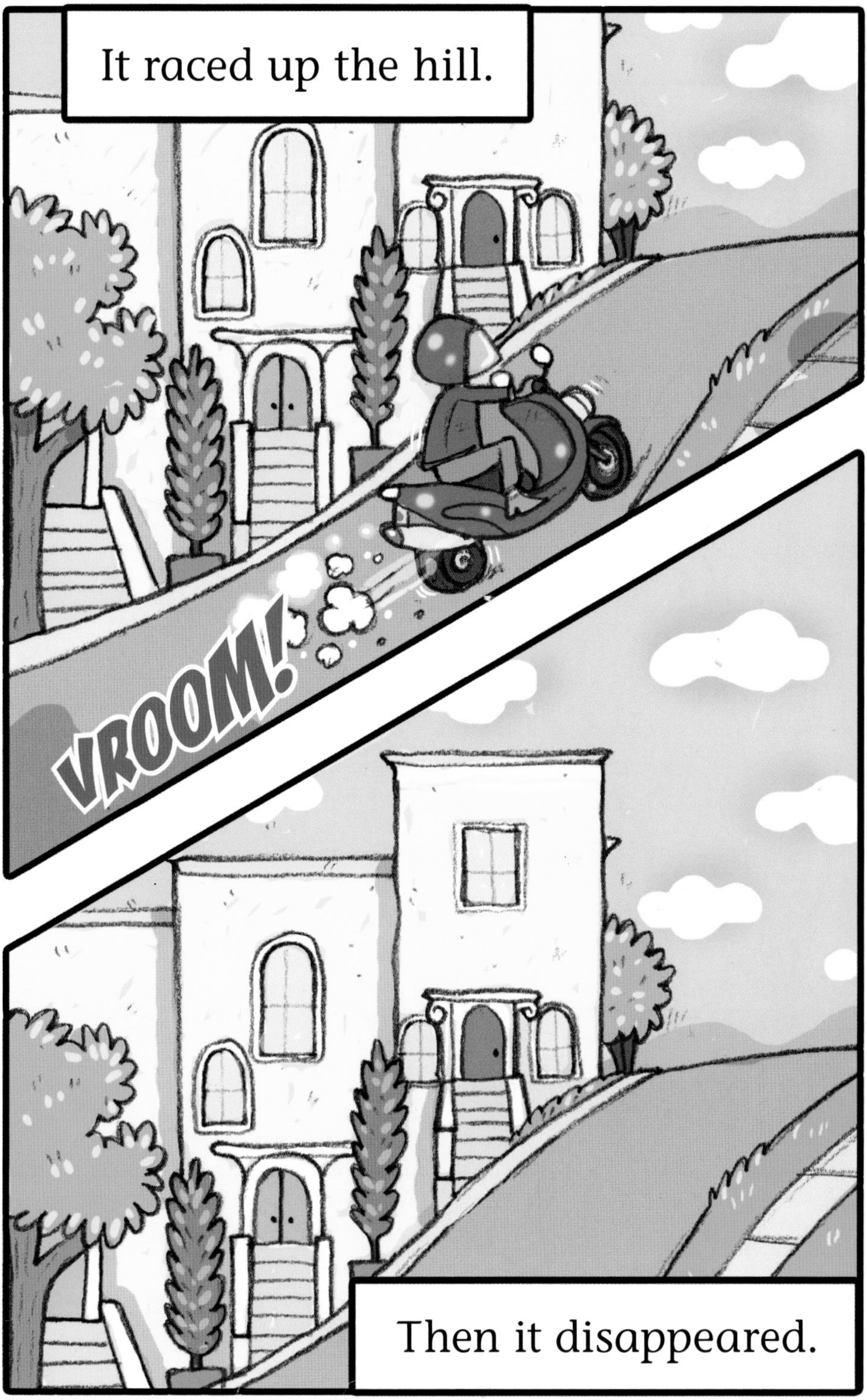
It raced up the hill.
VROOM!
Then it disappeared.

One day, Jackson was going to buy a scooter.

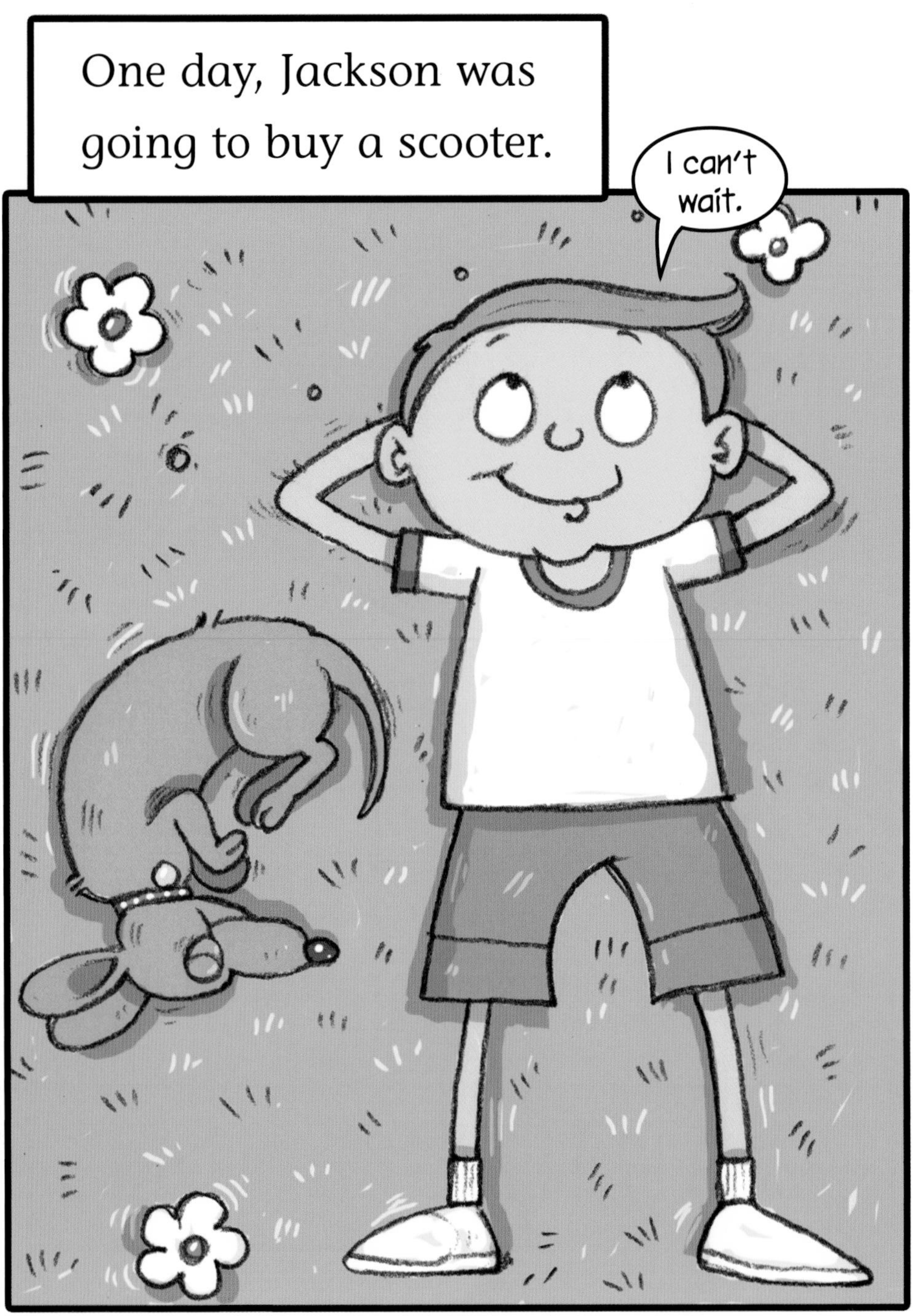
I can't wait.

It would be bright red. It would be extra shiny. It would be super fast.

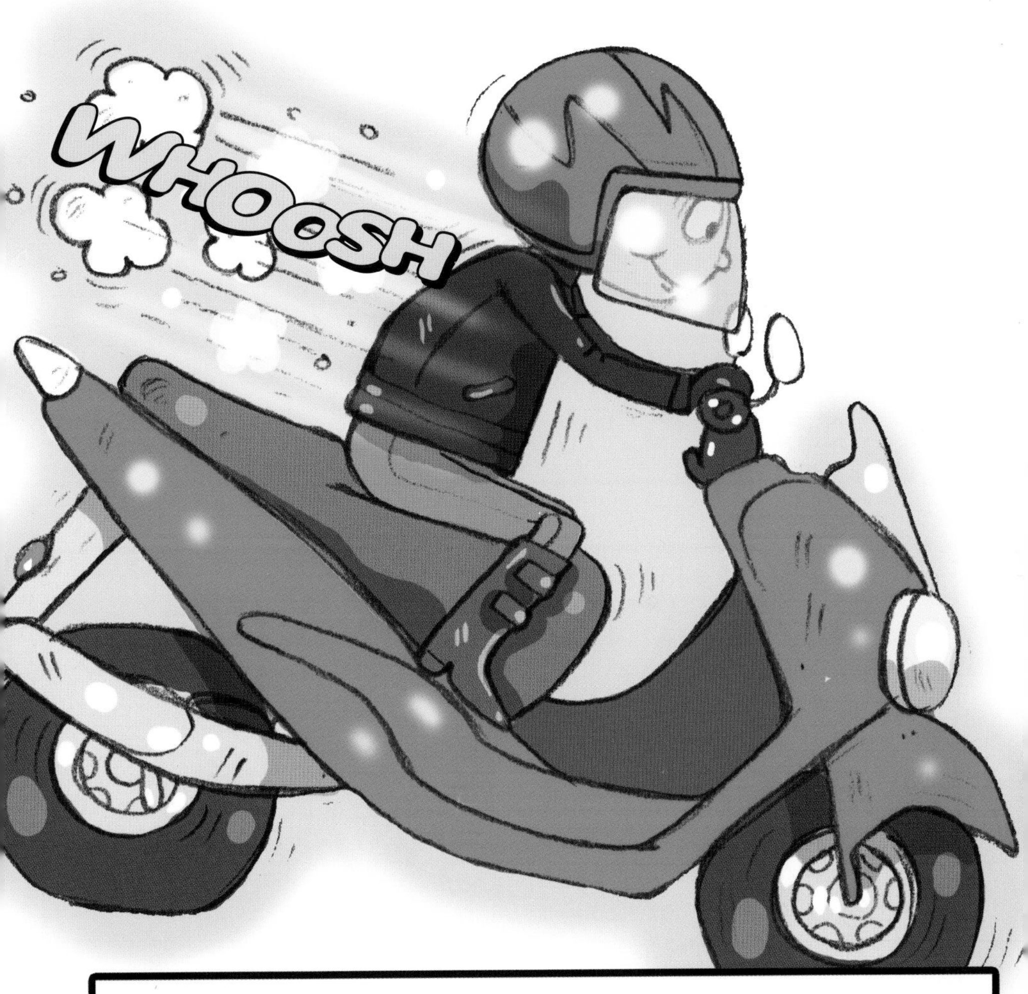
WHOOSH

It would be just like the shiny red blur.

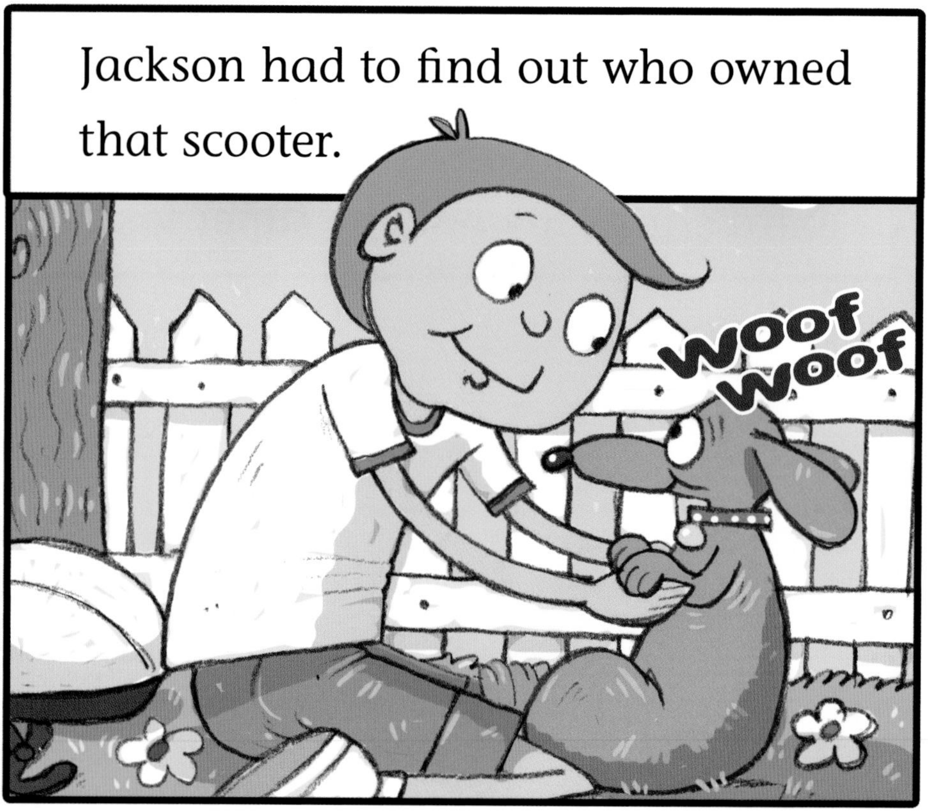
Jackson had to find out who owned that scooter.
WOOF WOOF

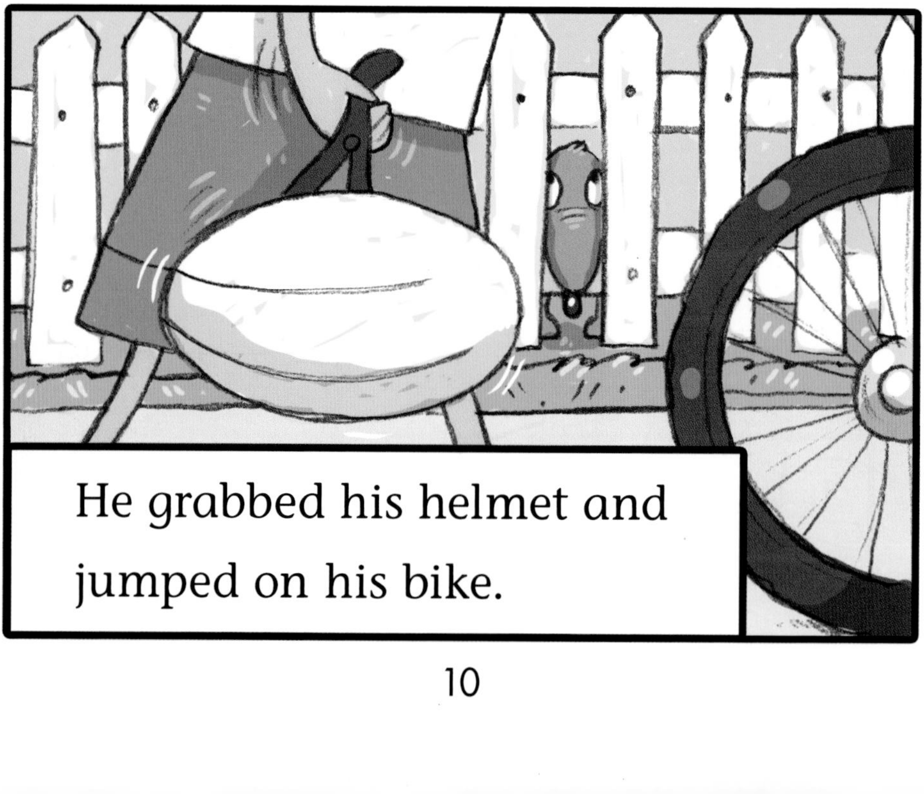
He grabbed his helmet and jumped on his bike.

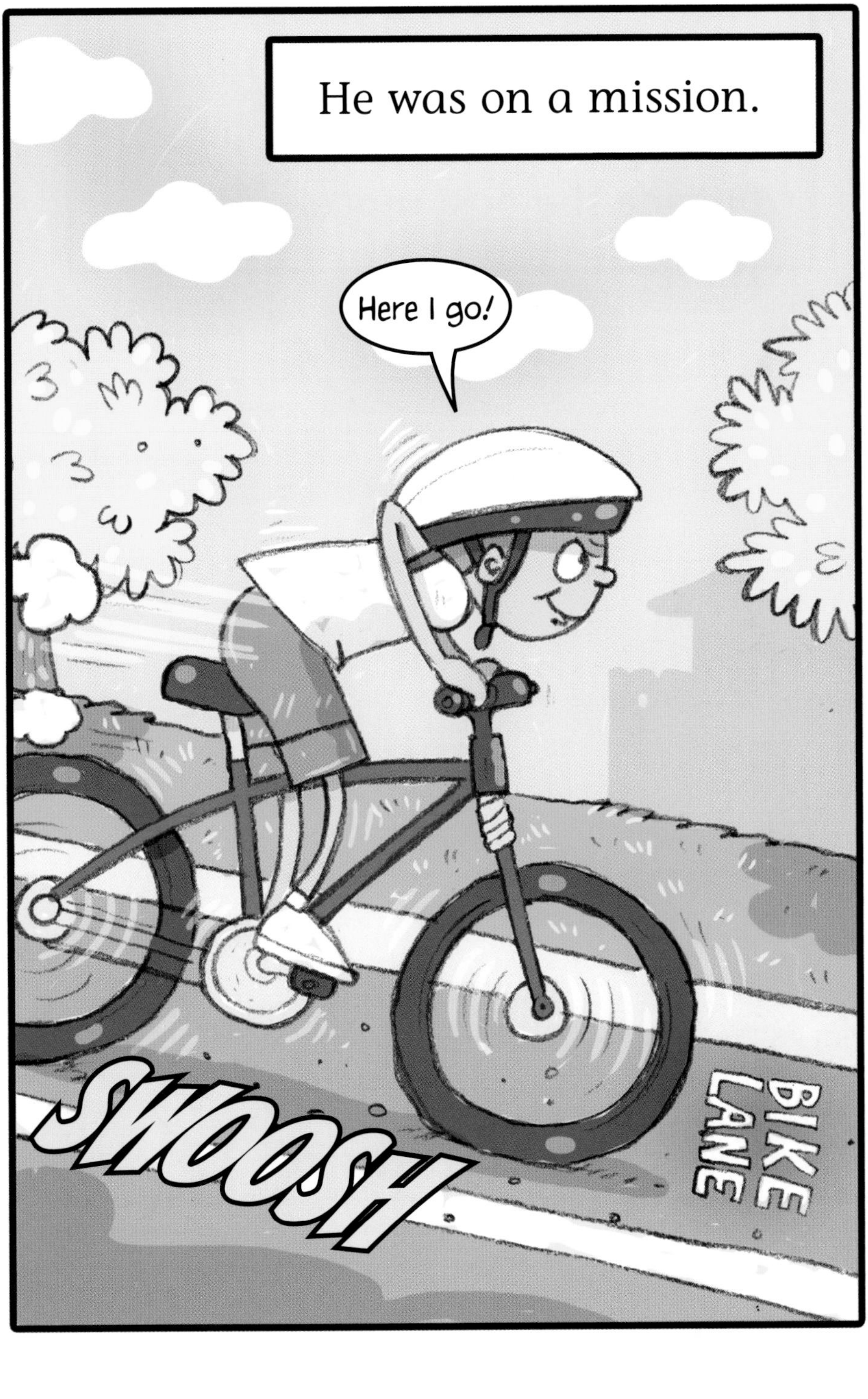
He was on a mission.
Here I go!
SWOOSH
BIKE LANE

As he zipped down the hill, he saw it. The scooter was parked outside the post office.

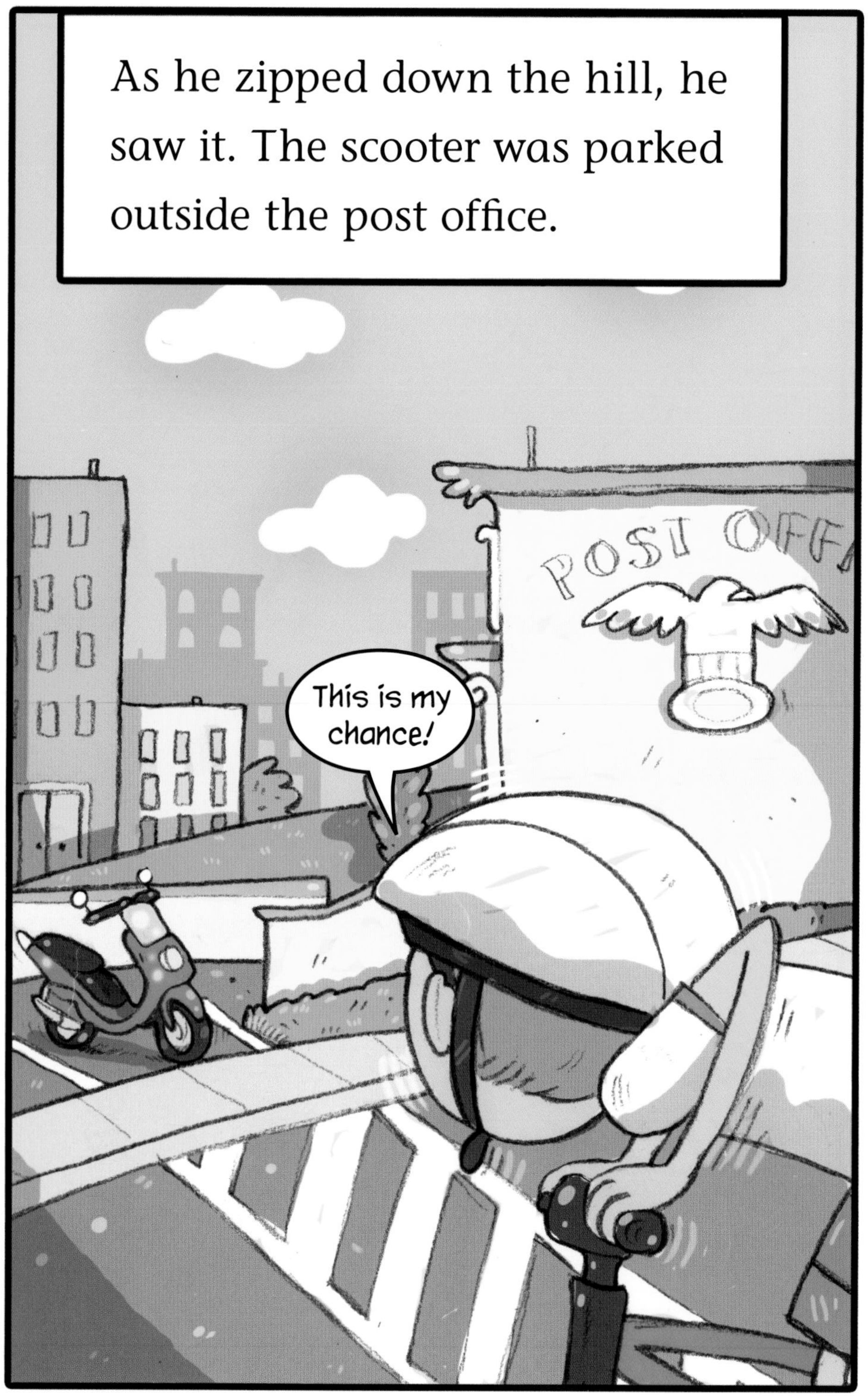

POST OFF
This is my chance!

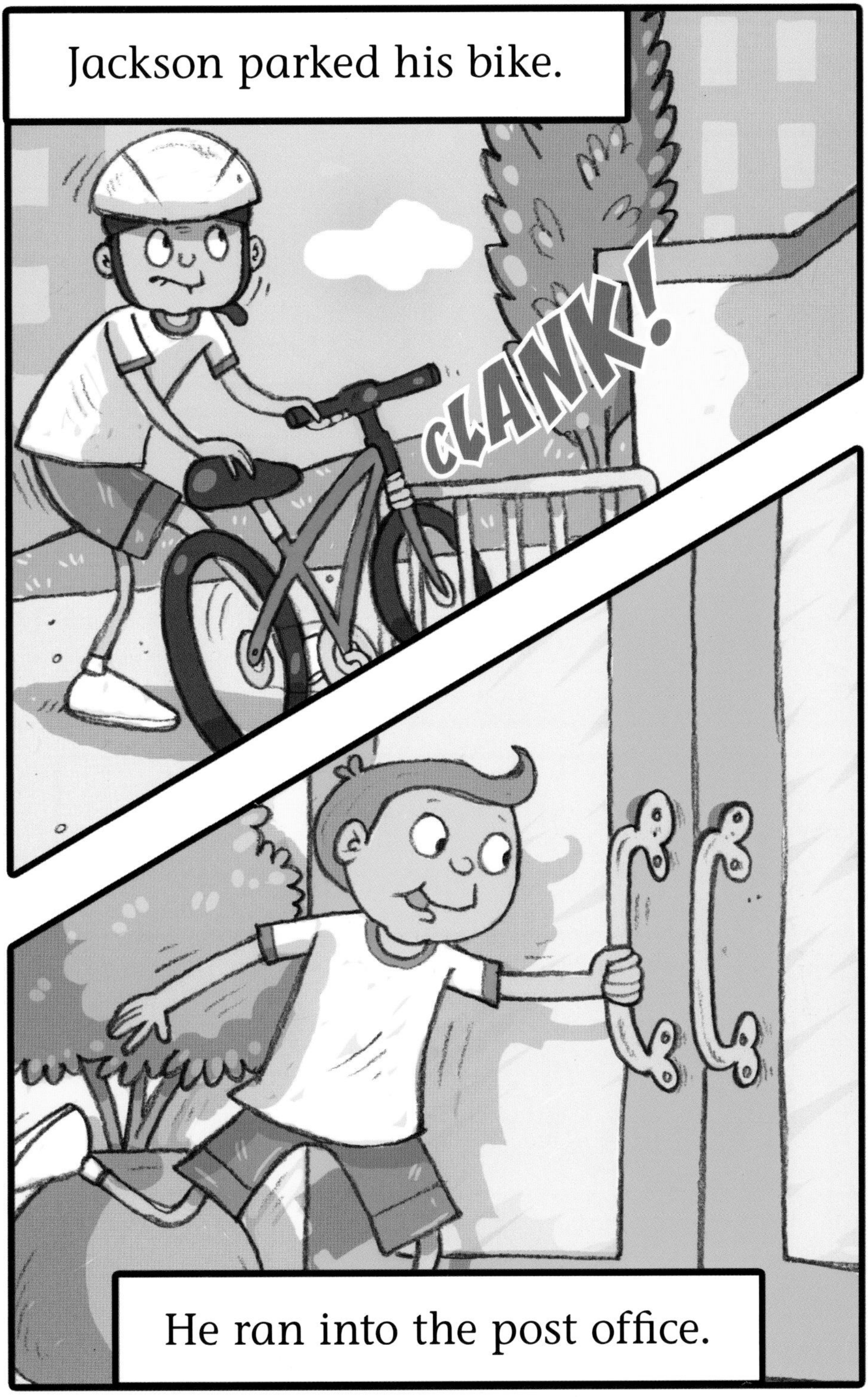
Jackson parked his bike.
CLANK!
He ran into the post office.

Then he bumped into his neighbor.

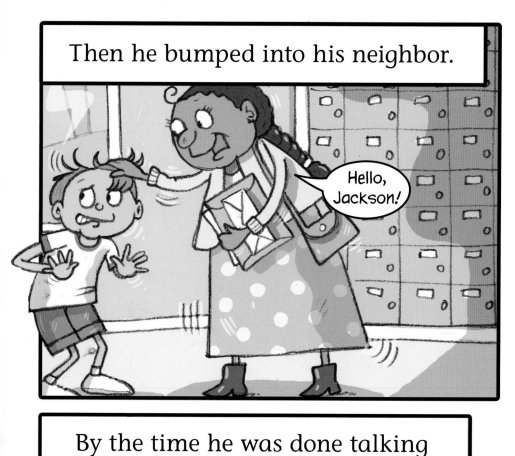

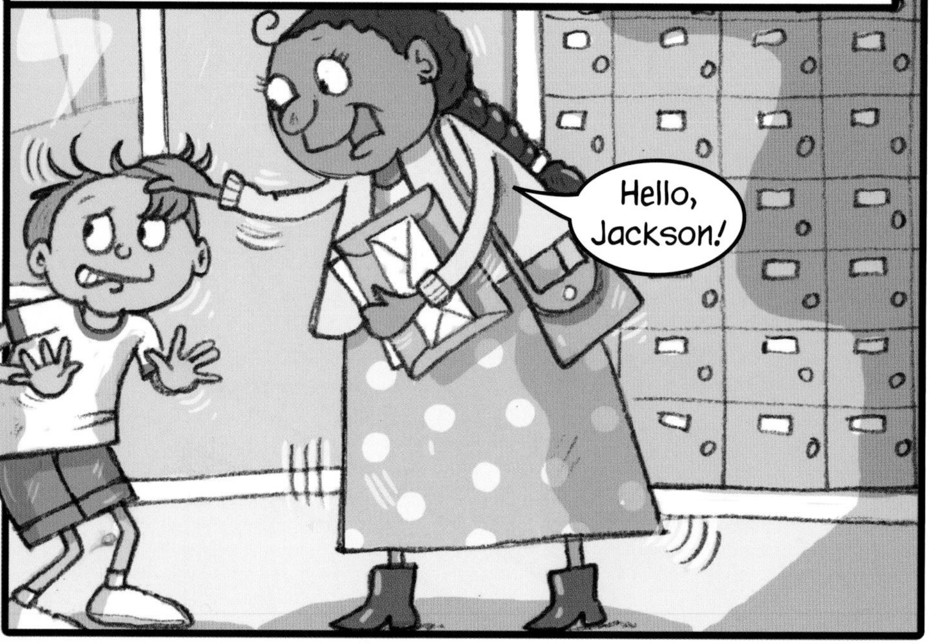
Hello,
Jackson!

By the time he was done talking to her, the scooter was leaving.

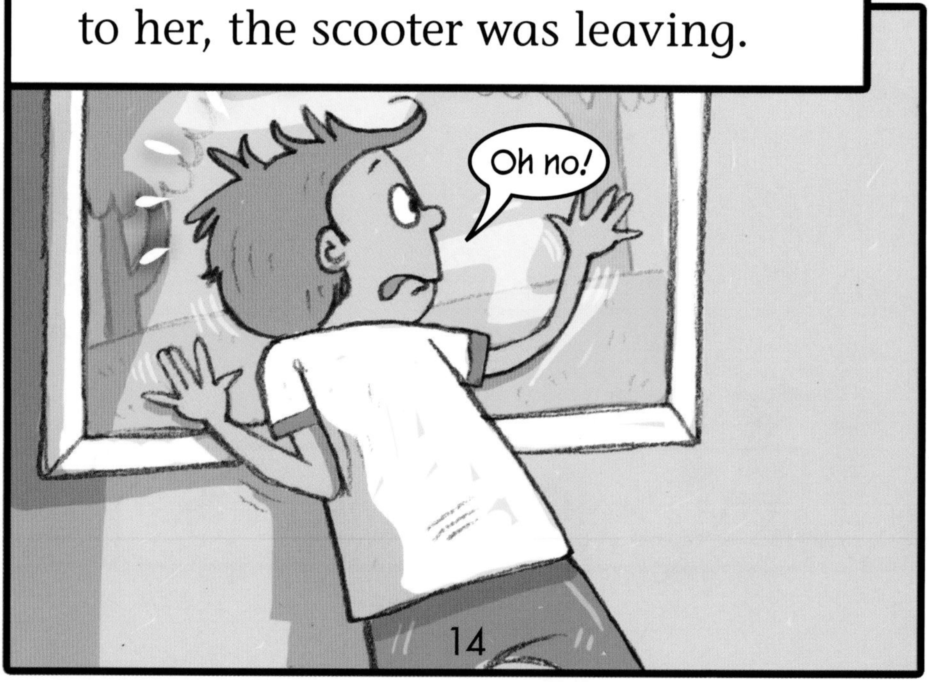
Oh no!

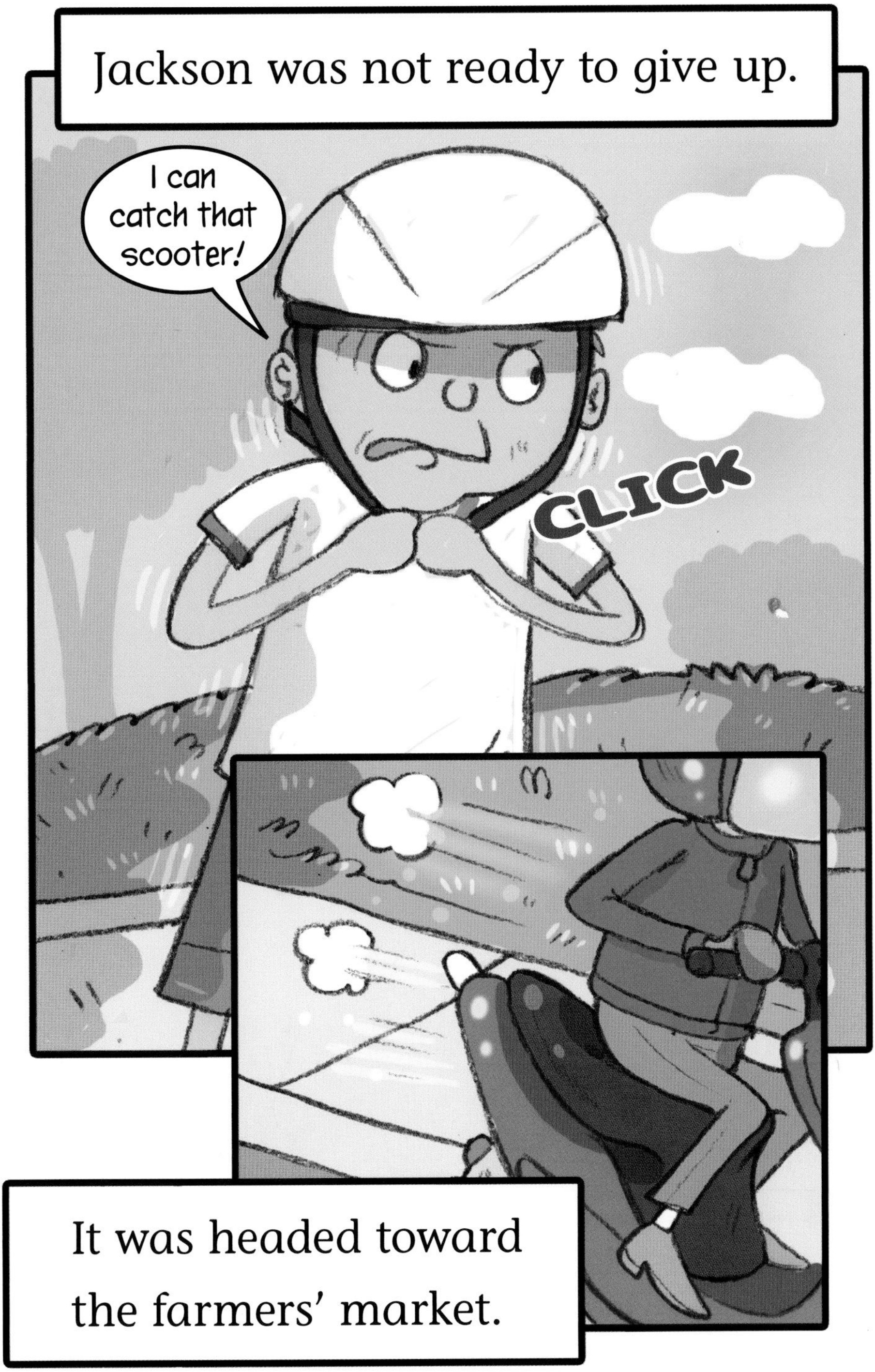
Jackson was not ready to give up.
I can catch that scooter!
CLICK
It was headed toward the farmers' market.

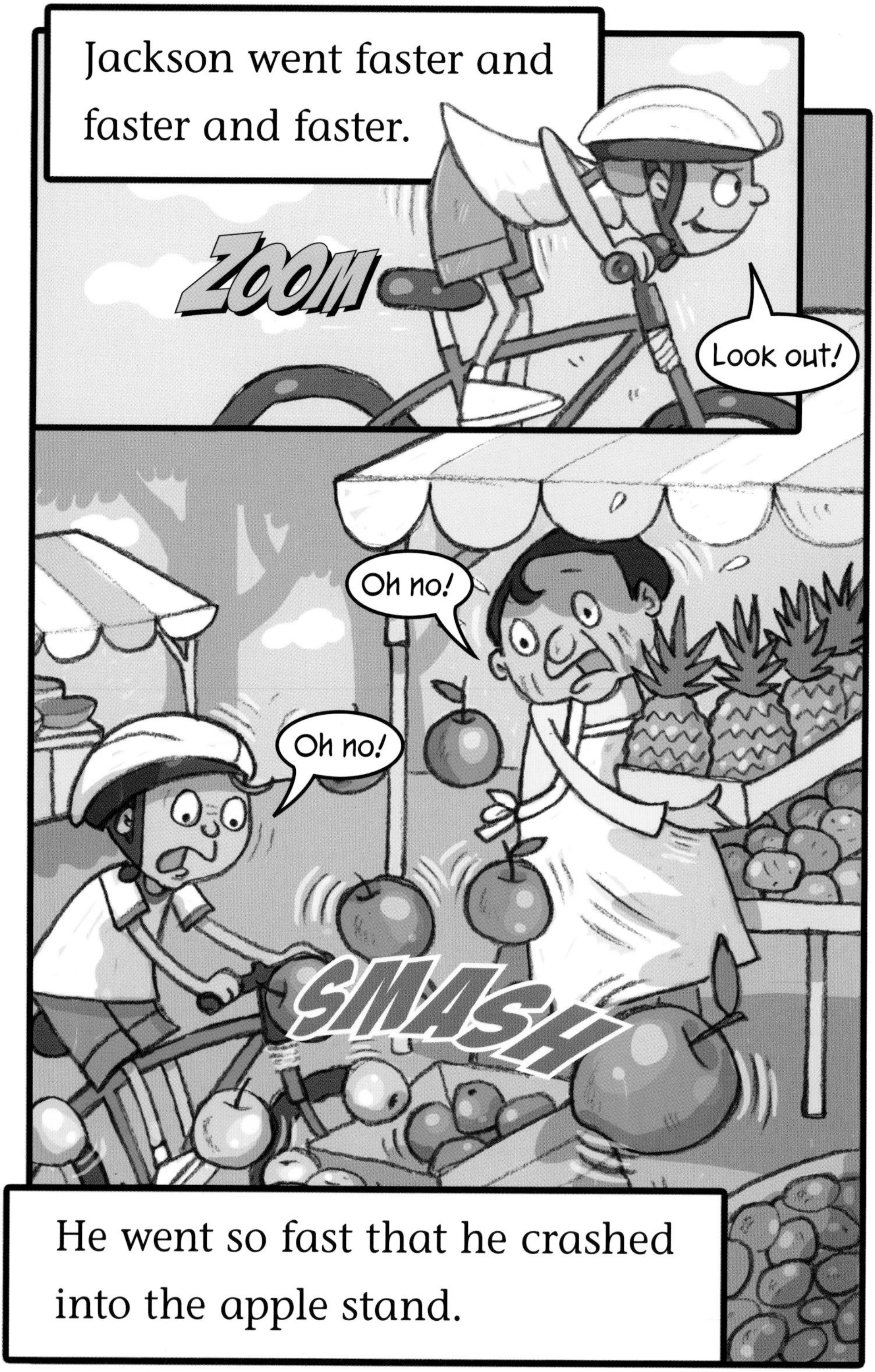
Jackson went faster and faster and faster.
ZOOM
Look out!
Oh no!
Oh no!
SMASH
He went so fast that he crashed into the apple stand.

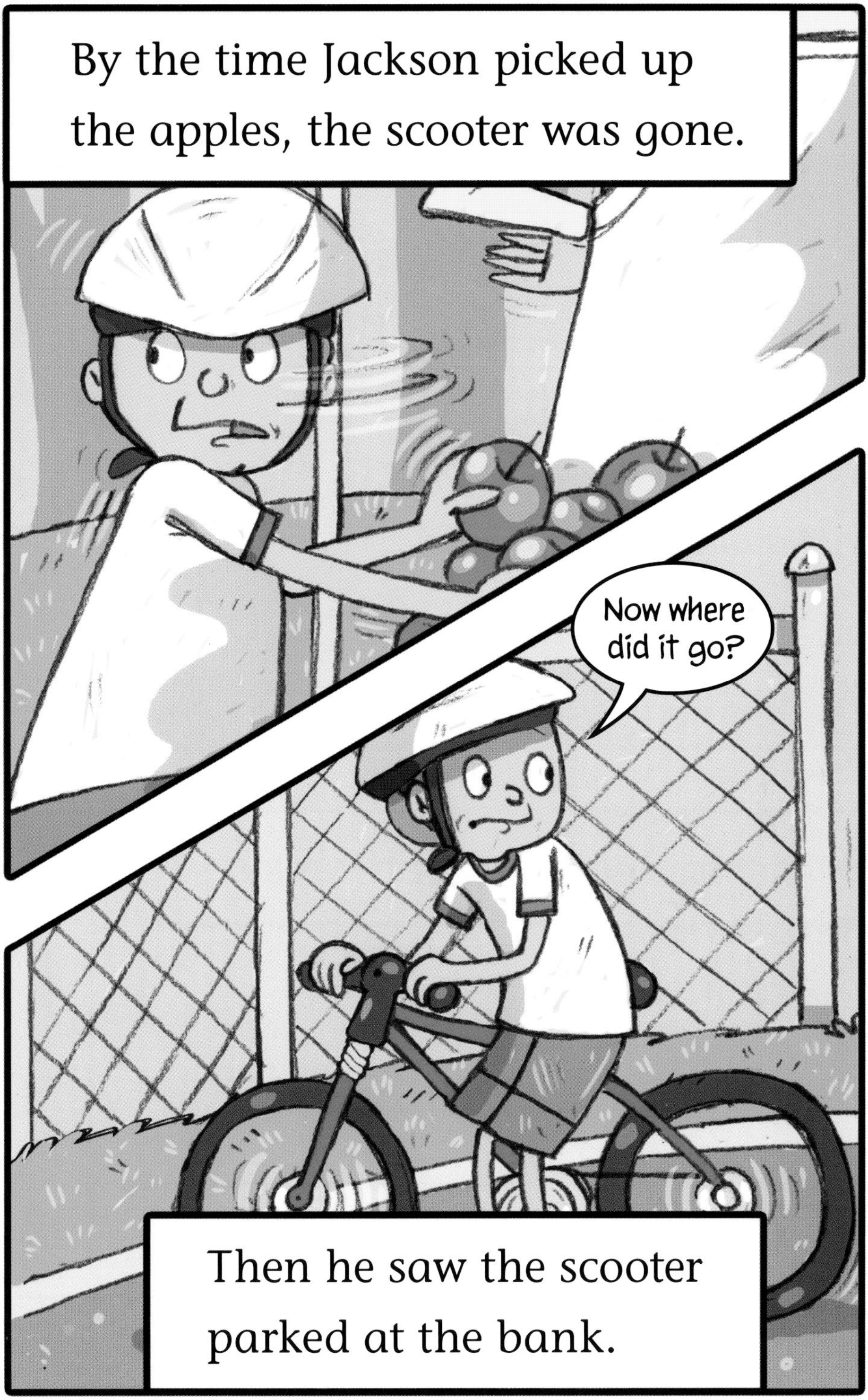
By the time Jackson picked up the apples, the scooter was gone.
Now where did it go?
Then he saw the scooter parked at the bank.

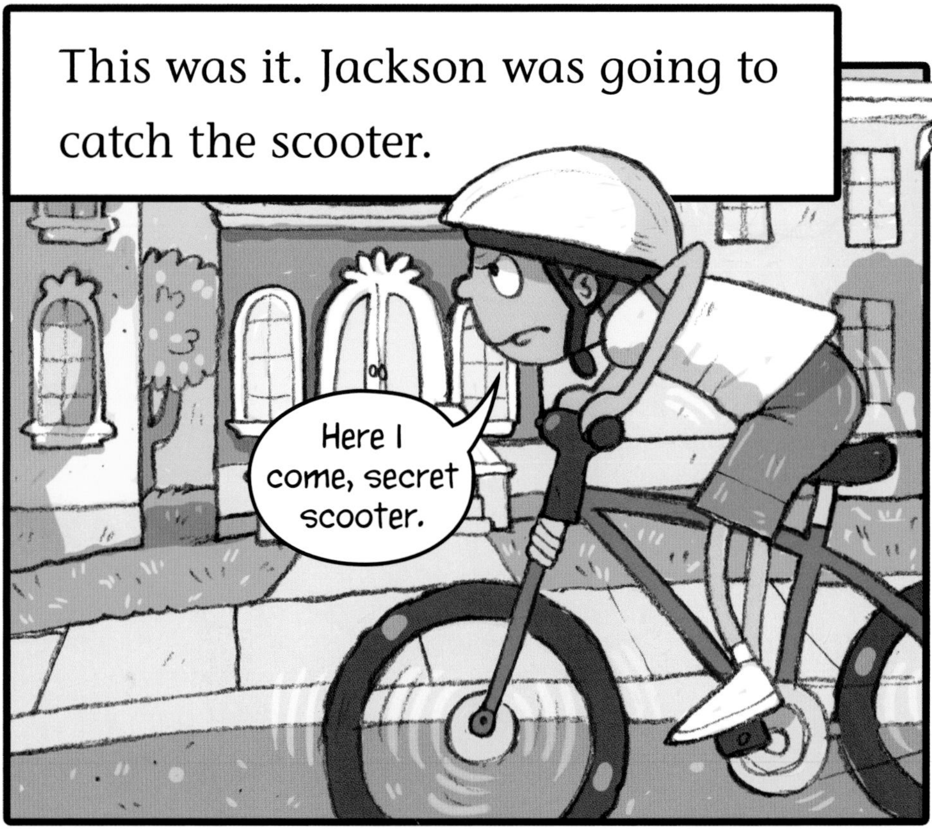
This was it. Jackson was going to catch the scooter.
Here I come, secret scooter.

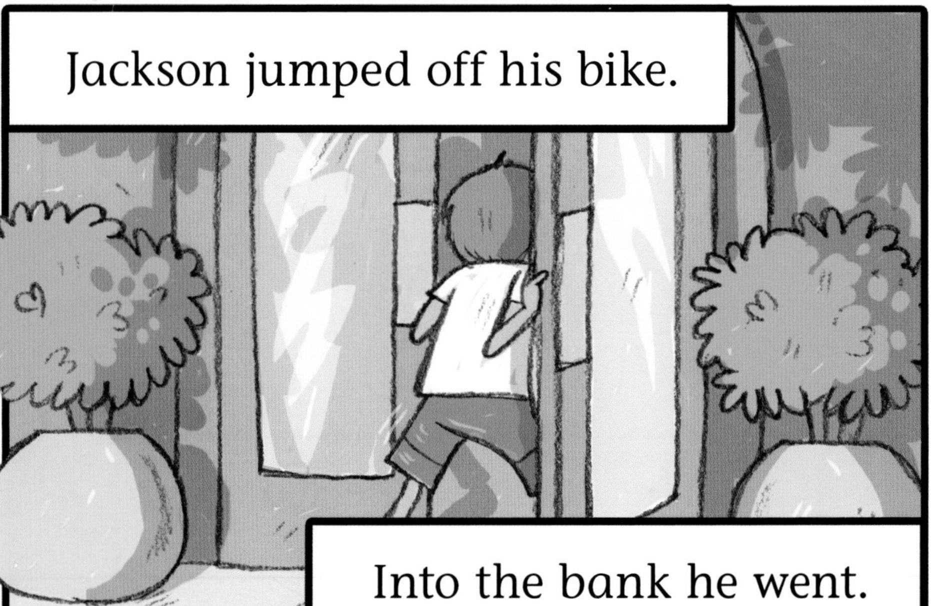
Jackson jumped off his bike.
Into the bank he went.

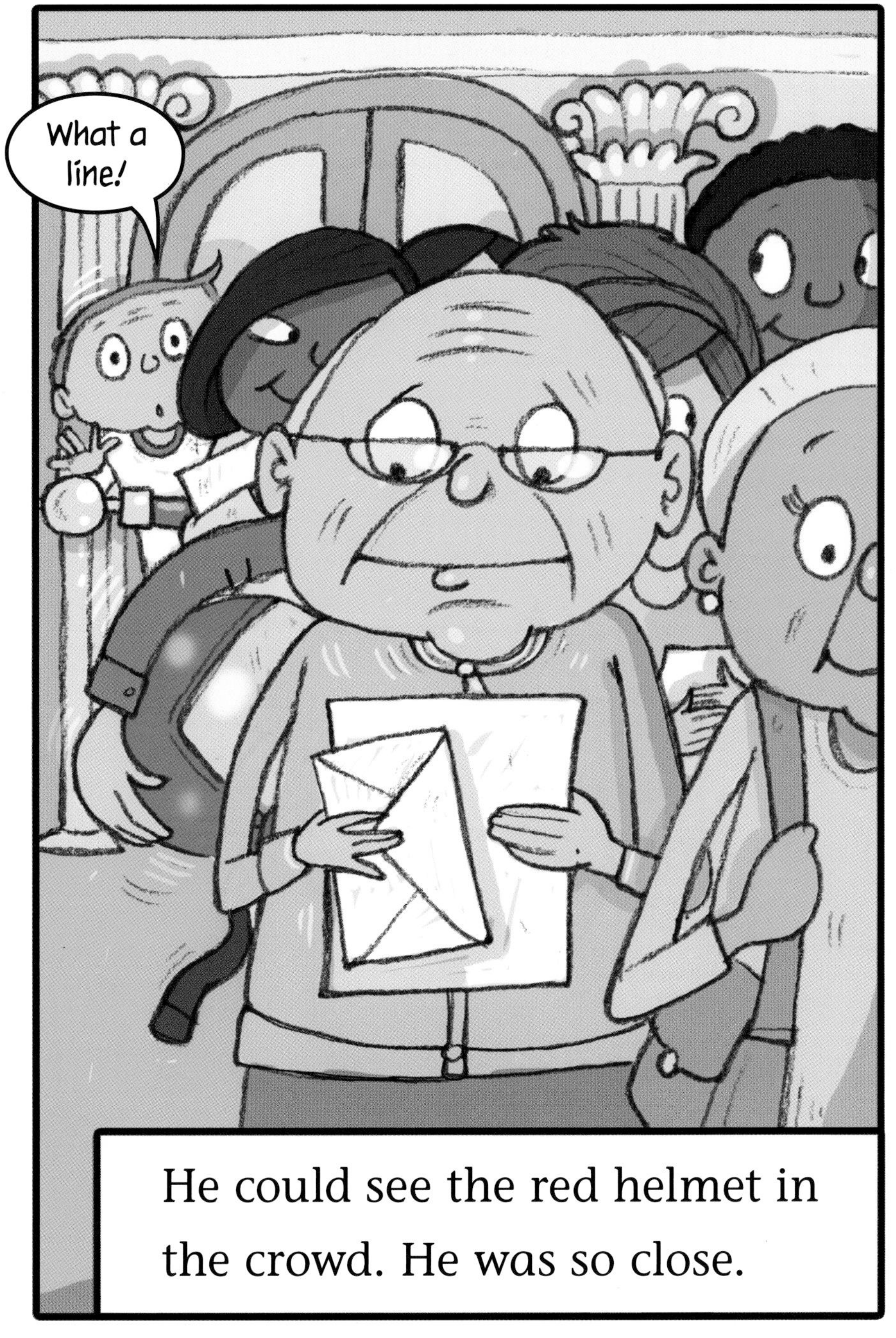
What a line!

He could see the red helmet in the crowd. He was so close.

Jackson tried a shortcut to get to the front of the line.

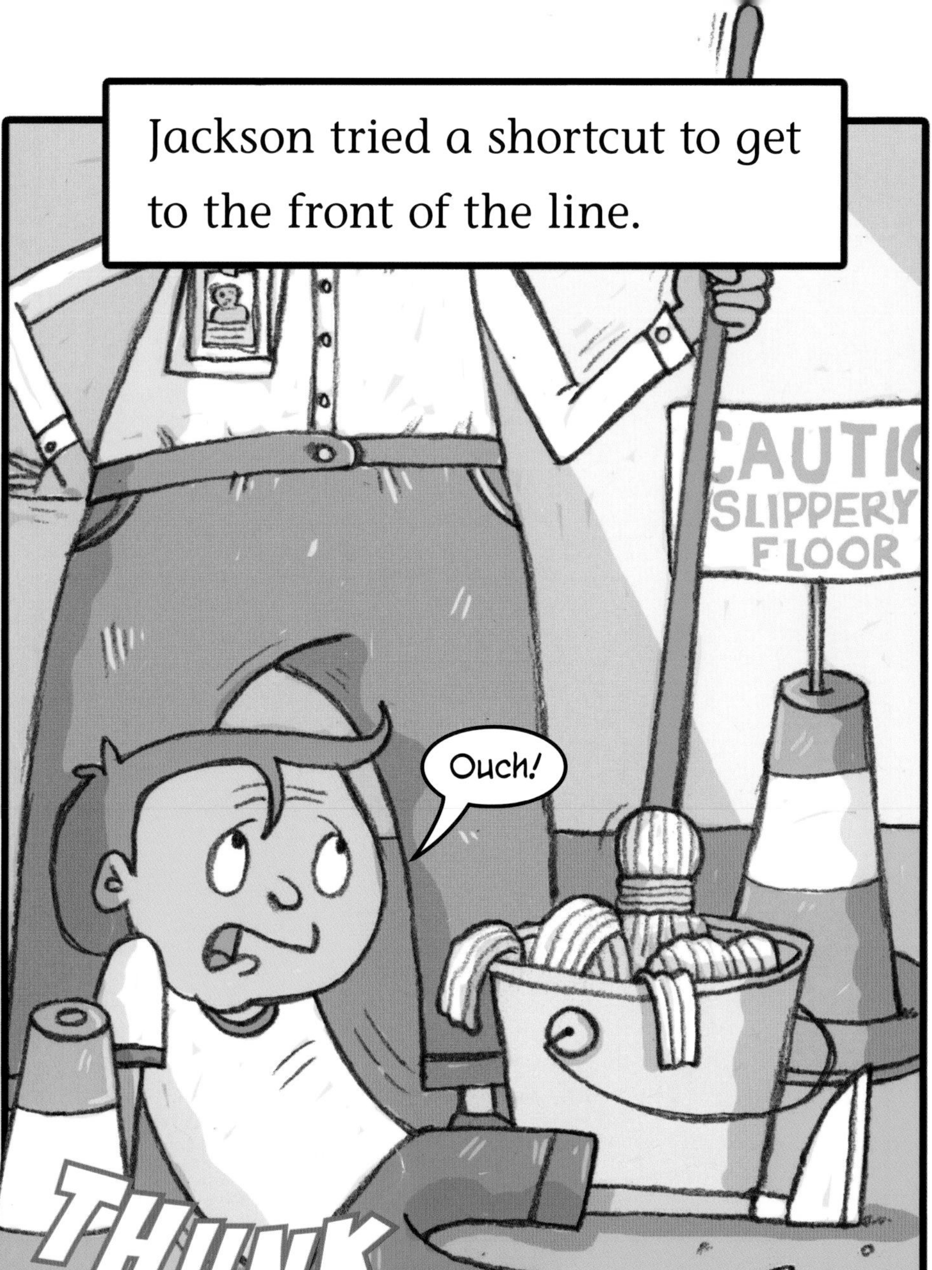
SLIPPERY
FLOOR
Ouch!
THUNK

But Jackson was not paying attention. He slipped and slid across the floor.

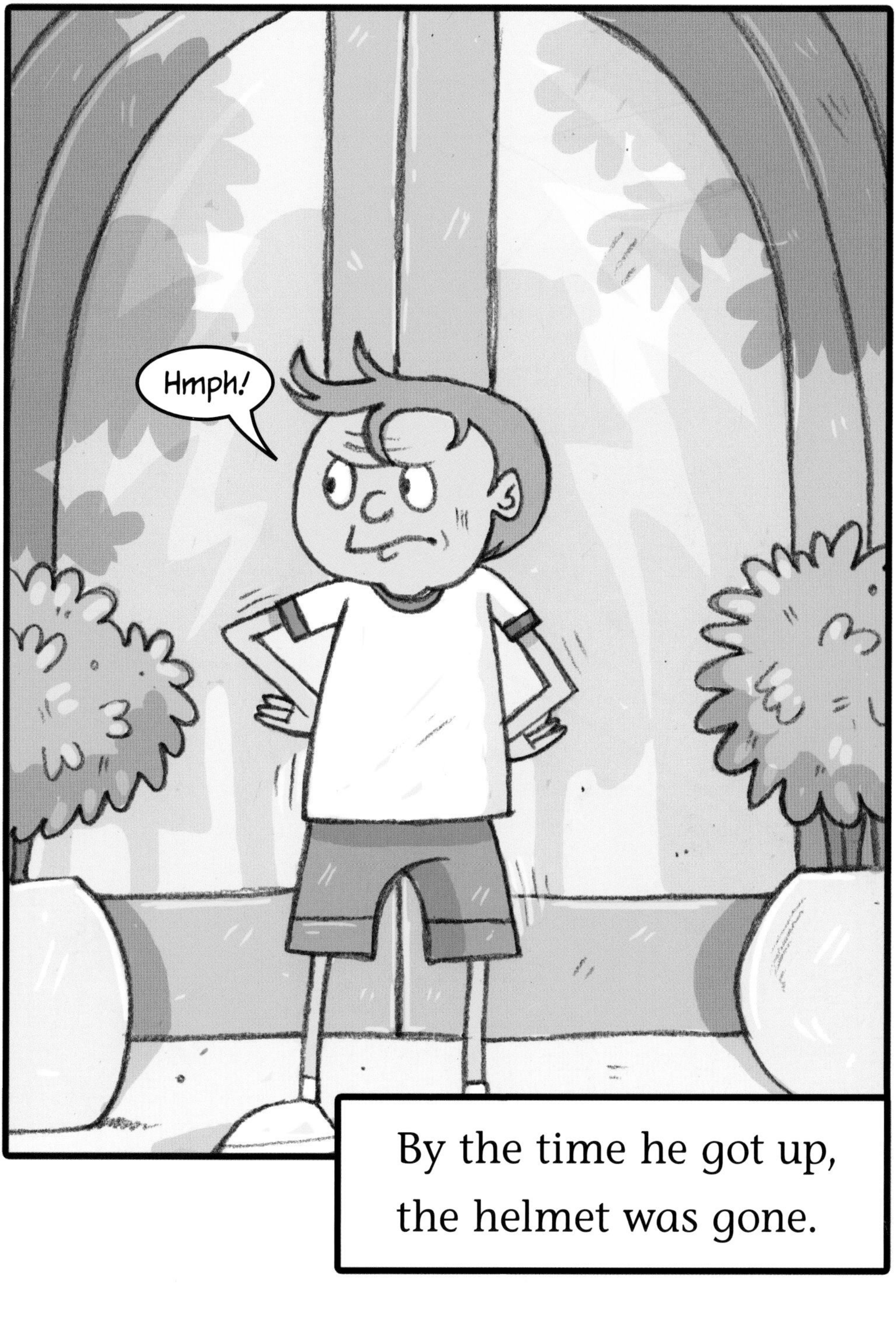
Hmph!

By the time he got up,
the helmet was gone.

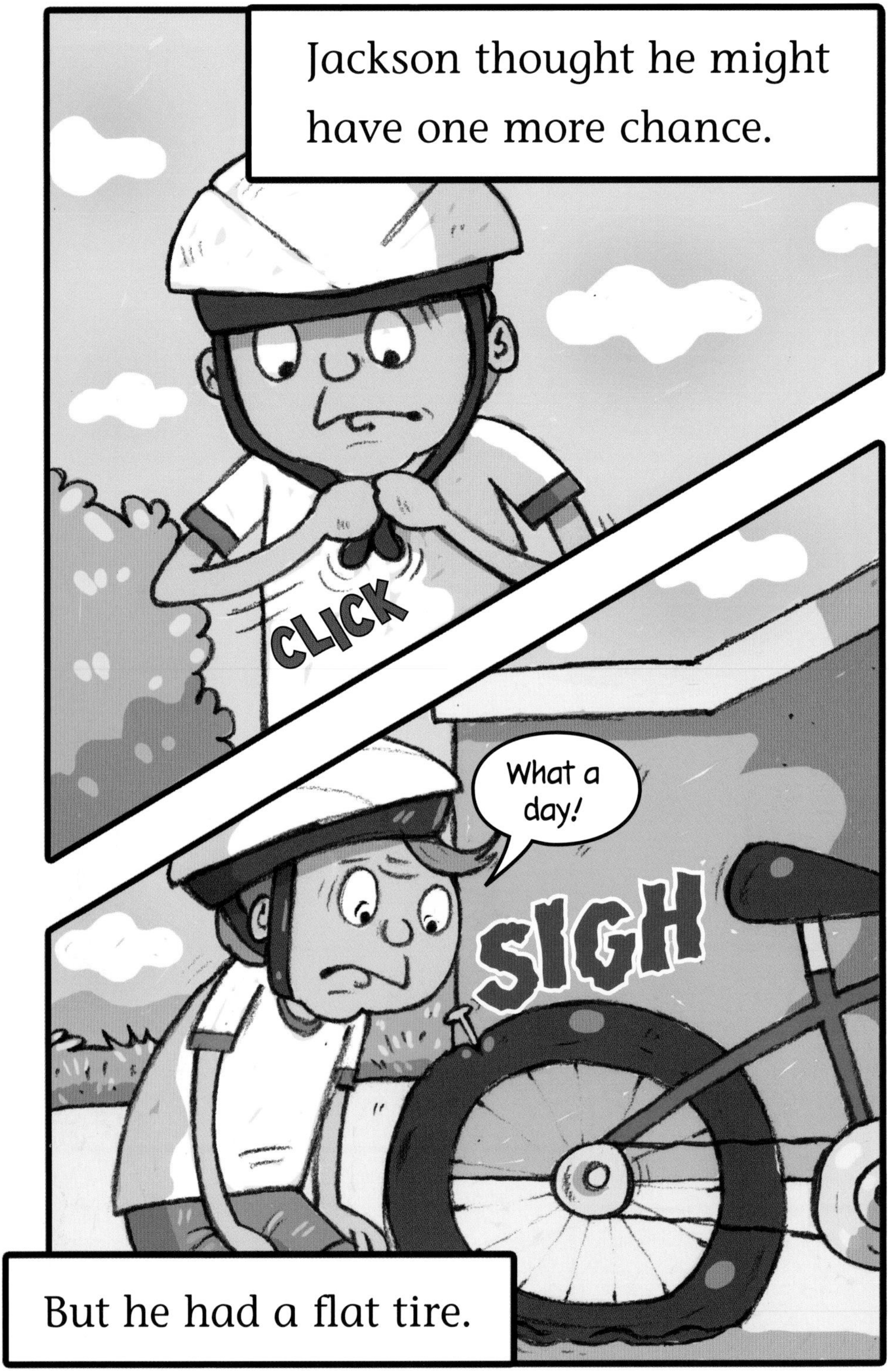
Jackson thought he might have one more chance.
CLICK
What a day!
SIGH
But he had a flat tire.

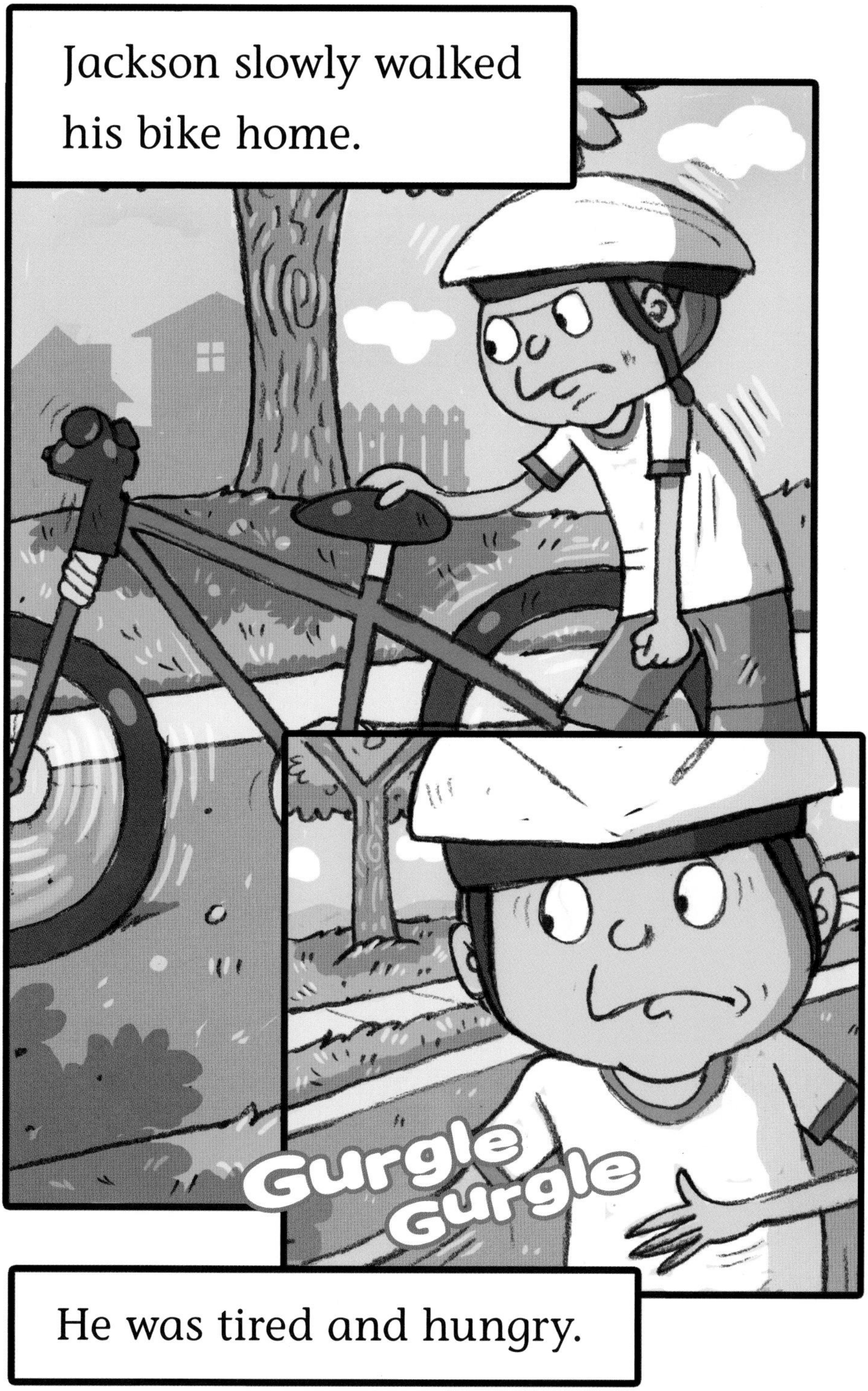
Jackson slowly walked his bike home.
Gurgle
Gurgle
He was tired and hungry.

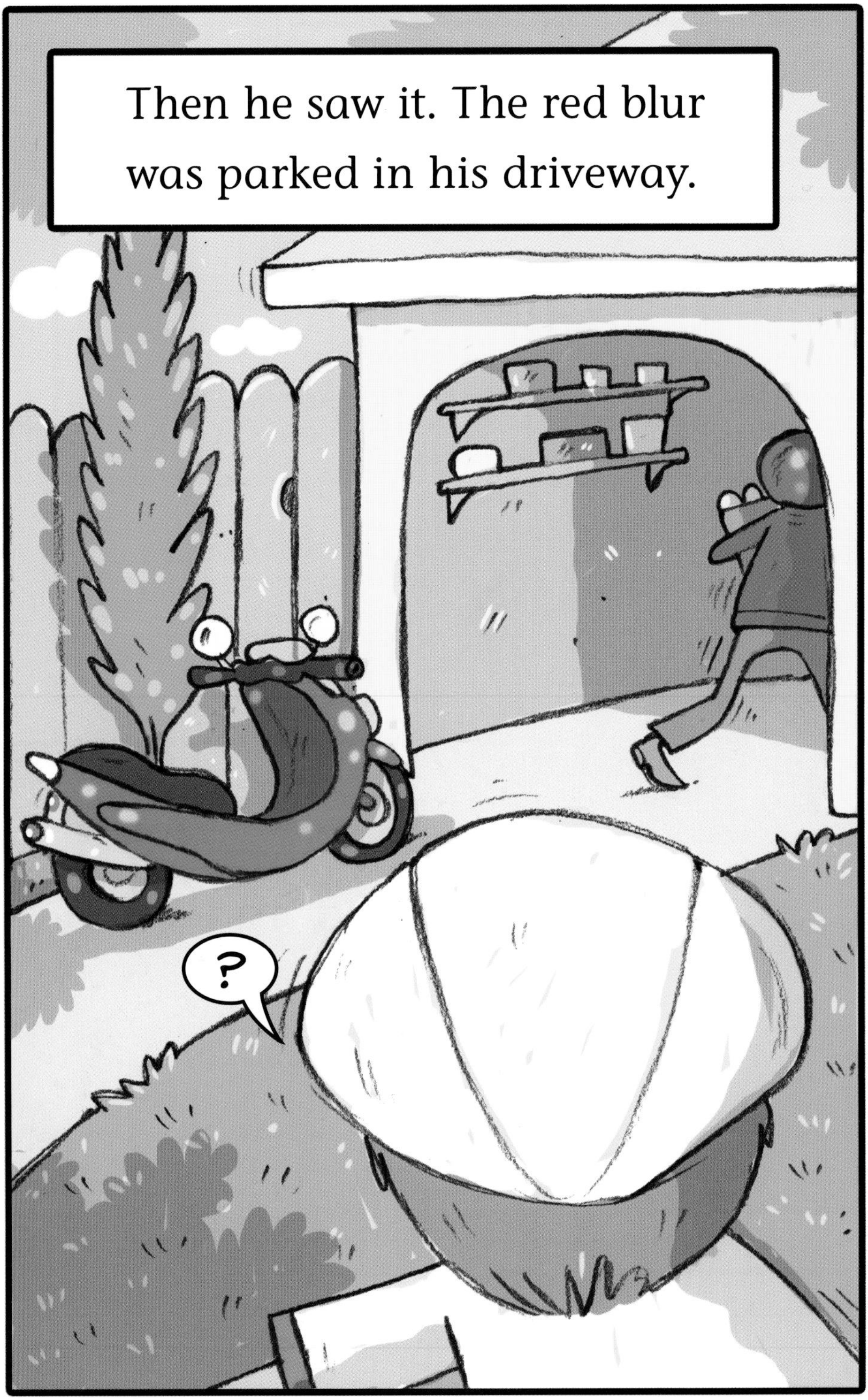
Then he saw it. The red blur was parked in his driveway.
?

And his mom was wearing the helmet.

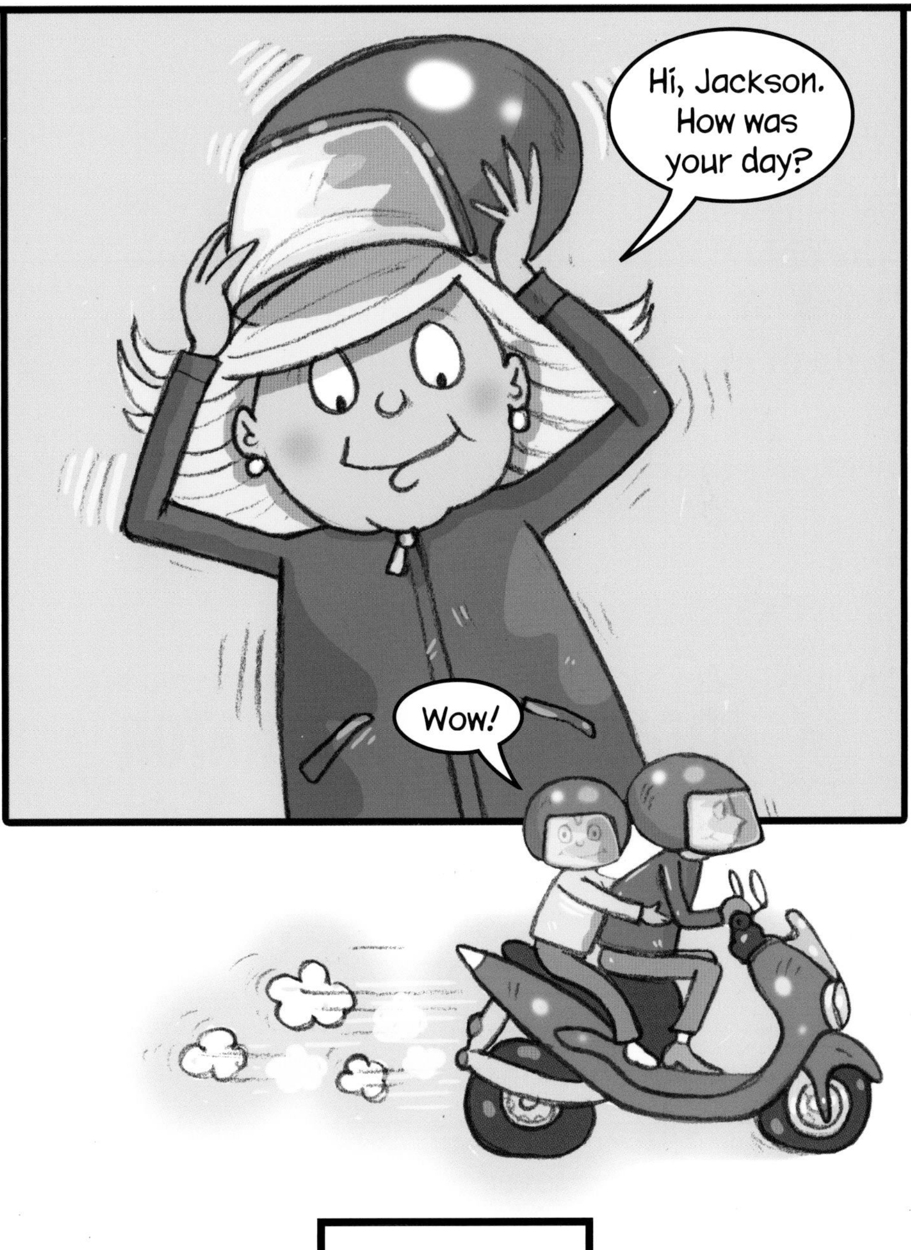
Hi, Jackson. How was your day?
Wow!

The End

ABOUT THE AUTHOR

Growing up in a small town with no cable TV (and parents who are teachers), reading was the only thing to do. Since then, Christianne Jones has read about a bazillion books and written more than 40. Christianne works as an editor and lives in Mankato, Minnesota, with her husband and daughter.

ABOUT THE ILLUSTRATOR

Mary Sullivan has been drawing and writing her whole life, which has mostly been spent in Texas. She earned a BFA from the University of Texas in Studio Art, but she considers herself a self-trained illustrator. Mary lives in Cedar Park, a suburb of Austin, Texas. She loves to go swimming in the lake with her dog.

GLOSSARY

blur (BLUR)—a shape that looks unclear because it's moving too fast

helmet (HEL-mit)—a hard hat that protects your head

mission (MISH-uhn)—a special job

scooter (SKOO-tur)—a small motorcycle

DISCUSSION QUESTIONS

1.) Jackson had quite an adventure trying to catch the scooter. Discuss an adventure you have had.

2.) Did you think Jackson would catch the scooter? Why or why not?

3.) Were you surprised by the ending of the story? Why or why not?

WRITING PROMPTS

1.) What if Jackson hadn't found the mystery scooter driver? Rewrite the ending of the book.

2.) If you had a scooter, what would it look like? Write a list of three things you would want your scooter to have.

3.) Throughout the book, there are sound and action words next to some of the pictures. Pick at least two of those words. Then write your own sentences using those words.

THE 1ST STEP INTO GRAPHIC NOVELS

These books are the perfect introduction to graphic novels. Combine an entertaining story with comic book panels, exciting action elements, and bright colors, and a safe graphic novel is born.

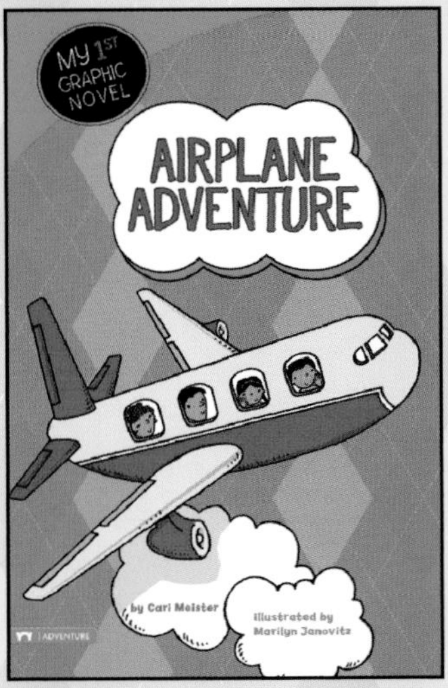
MY 1ST GRAPHIC NOVEL
AIRPLANE ADVENTURE
by Cari Meister
illustrated by Marilyn Janovitz
ADVENTURE

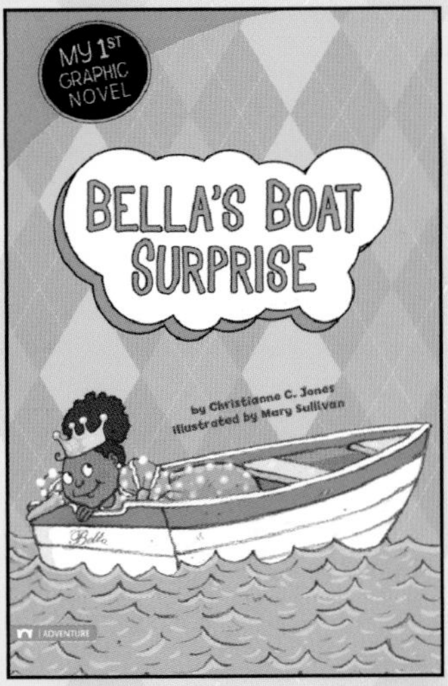
MY 1ST GRAPHIC NOVEL
BELLA'S BOAT SURPRISE
by Christianne C. Jones
illustrated by Mary Sullivan
ADVENTURE

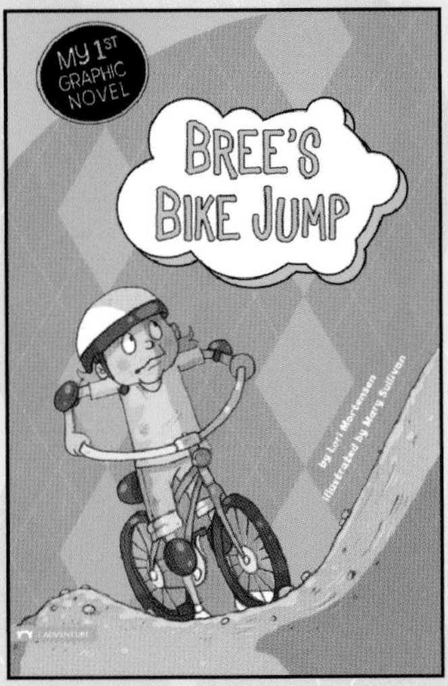
MY 1ST GRAPHIC NOVEL
BREE'S BIKE JUMP
ADVENTURE

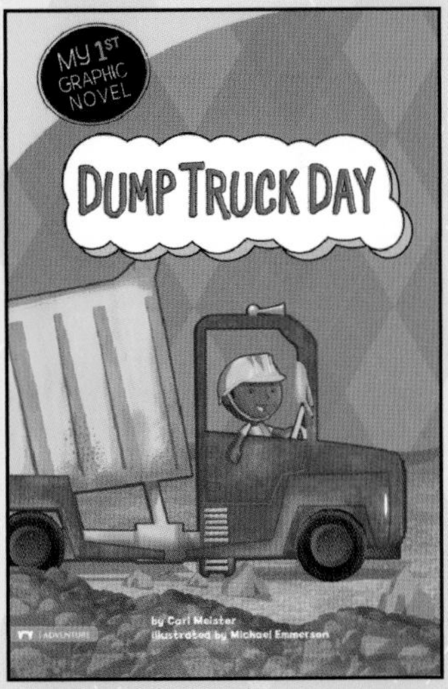
MY 1ST GRAPHIC NOVEL
DUMP TRUCK DAY
by Cari Meister
illustrated by Michael Emmerson
ADVENTURE

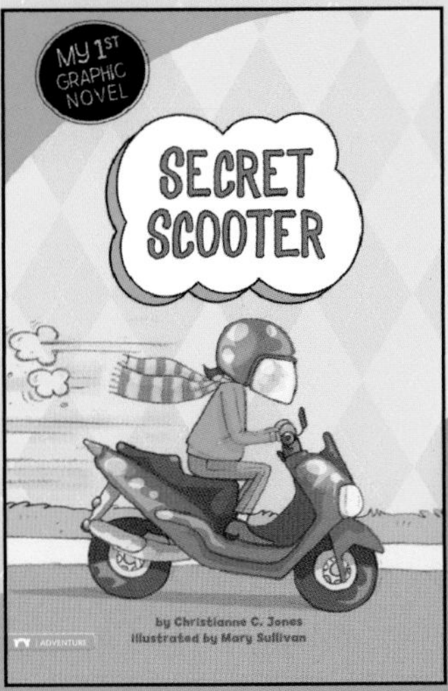
MY 1ST GRAPHIC NOVEL
SECRET SCOOTER
by Christianne C. Jones
illustrated by Mary Sullivan
ADVENTURE

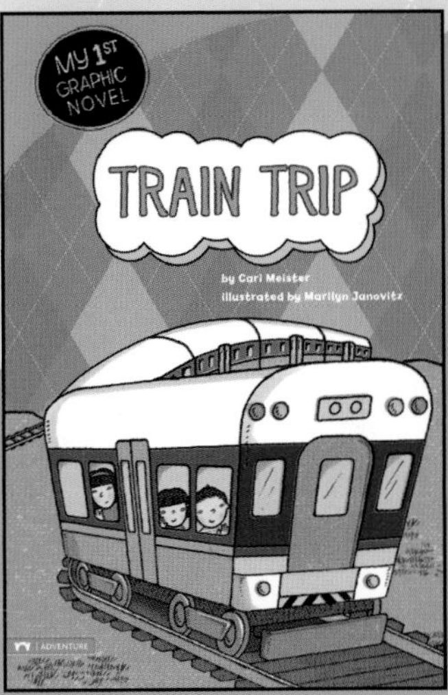
MY 1ST GRAPHIC NOVEL
TRAIN TRIP
by Cari Meister
illustrated by Marilyn Janovitz
ADVENTURE